EARTHQUAKE

EARTH

TURTLE POINT PRESS NEW YORK

Susan Barnes

QUAKE

Earthquake was originally published
in a limited handset letterpress edition
by Turtle Point Press in 1990.

Copyright © 2007 by Susan Barnes
Copyright © 2007 by Turtle Point Press

ISBN-13: 978-1-933527-11-6
ISBN-10: 1-933527-11-0
LCCN: 2006906983

Design and composition by Jeff Clark at
Wilsted & Taylor Publishing Services

TO MIMI

CONTENTS

EARTHQUAKE

THE BOAT

An unused boat had been propped up off the damp ground by two logs at each end. It was there for a long time before I rolled it over and slipped it through the reeds and took it downriver. At first I'd lie under it in the moss and fall asleep. In the dreams objects were repositioned. The boat was turned over and moved to the river, and I was in a sitting position in it. The river was wider. No rocks, no reeds, no banks, just water.

My sister and I went to school with a girl who had a teenage sister. Once we were invited over after school. Patty's sister looked like a woman, but she ran around just as we did, in fact better. Pam used to take her Siamese cat and throw it into a pond. She'd say, "You've got to hear this!" and grab the cat and take off out the door. Linda, Patty, and I were half her size. Pam ran like an animal. The cat screamed in the air. My sister and I had never seen a cat in air. It was all claws and eyes. "Watch!" Pam said, shoving up her jacket sleeves. The cat sank between concentric circles and emerged after a long time somewhere else. It was trying to get over the place where water met air, but it was not swimming. It was as if the cat were constantly stepping onto a table that was not there. "She does this all the time," Patty said, throwing a mud ball onto a boulder and making it splat. "C'mon, let's go. I hate you Pam." We waited until the cat was on shore and had disappeared in a heap of old car parts. Later that year, when my father's hunting partner brought over his two teenage sons, my sister Linda threw our cat into the air. Luckily the river was frozen. The boys said, "What'd you do that for?" Linda just stood there with her mouth open. Then she said, "I was just checking the ice."

•

Coffee cans were just the right size for carrying containers while wading through marshlands. Once, while I was collecting leeches off my boots, I saw a bullfrog on a rock open his mouth and pull a mosquito in with a stone-white tongue. I caught the frog and tried to feed it leeches. He urinated and kept his mouth shut. I held still so mosquitos would come for me and showed them to him, but he wasn't interested. I wanted to see his tongue. I held insects by their wings near him. I tried water skaters, spiders, and snails. He wouldn't let me see. I dropped the can and rubbed his belly. He lay limp in my hand for a while, but when I tried to slip my finger between his jaws, he came back to frog shape. When I squeezed him accidentally because he was getting away, I saw his mouth open slightly. I figured squeezing was the only way in. I already had a wart, so I put him back in the can and used a rock. The rock was too big or I pressed too hard. When I got the rock out, the frog was dead. I had broken its back. I carried him around in my jacket pocket and checked every once in a while. It was always the same thing—the frog I had killed.

First time I saw oars used was in Tee Harbor. For a while my parents were caretakers of a cedar-and-glass house built into the side of the cliffs. It was an area of shore where the difference between high tide and low tide was extreme. One day my sister and I went out at low tide with cans and sticks. Sometimes the only way to tell a plant from an animal in a tide pool is to poke it with a stick. I don't know how it happened, except that we were mostly looking down, but once we made it all the way out. Rocks the size of houses stood in irregular groups, like guardians of the water . . . like slow, whispering animals. The ones up close hissed with barnacles and steamed in the sun. Long seaweed arms flapped about in the wind. We took ahold and climbed up. After a while my sister went back to the house for crackers, and I fell asleep. She forgot about me, and the tide came in. It was all the way up to the top of the rock when I woke up. I held on to the seaweed. Waves covered the world between bows the sea made. My mother and sisters were on the shore waving. The only connection between their bodies and mine was visual. When waves rose, I lost them. When it was mostly blue, something orange began showing up. It was the man who lived on top of the cliff. A writer, my mother had told us. He had seen me with his binoculars and came out with his rubber dinghy. That's when I learned about rowing. I watched him rowing up and down mountainous waves from the floor of that boat. I saw how the oars were fastened so cleverly into loose rings.

There was so much iron in the soil it turned the river around our house in the woods orange. The sediment around the reeds and at the bottom of the river was also orange. The mark that boat made on its way out through the reeds was almost red. I got good with oars and water, and I knew where certain animals lived. At first the beavers slapped the water with their tails and the bears just watched. But after a while they just did what they do—carry logs or chew. Black bears and deer ate from bushes, beavers from trees. Grizzlies ate salmon. I didn't see a grizzly often, but when I did, I'd pick up the oars and let the boat drift. Grizzlies had a game of throwing the fish high into the air so they arched and glistened in the sun before they were swallowed whole or pulled apart with a paw on rock.

My mother took us swimming a few times in the lake around the Mendenhall Glacier. It was our favorite activity. There were not that many days warm enough to do it. Once, on a particularly warm day, we saw the lake was thick and black when we arrived. It had been thickened with tadpoles. Linda and I went in anyway with our inner tubes, but it wasn't water, so we got out.

The generator shed made strange noises. My father warned us to stay away from it. The kennel room where my father operated on animals was also out-of-bounds, and so were the top and bottom drawers of my parents' dresser. It all made complete sense. I knew exactly where to go to shut down the electricity, to make an incision, to get a gun, and to take money.

My father's questions at the dinner table were often the same every night: "What'd you see today, Susan?"

"A hawk take a rabbit up over Linda's hill and drop it and catch it again in air. From the boat I saw the beavers, deer, bear, and bobcat. I saw green frogs. I found some bones. I don't know what. I'll show you, I got them. I saw blue jays and crows."

"What kind of bear?" he asked, cutting moose with his jackknife because it worked better than the table one.

"Grizzly."

He nodded. "You put vinegar on this?" he asked my mother. "That wasn't a grizzly, Susan."

"Daddy, I know bears. It was. He plays the fish game. I see him a lot, I told you."

"It wasn't a grizzly. This is kind of tough," he said of the meat. "Doesn't that boat leak? You didn't see any bears," he said. Then he talked with my mother about people I didn't know. After a while he put down his silverware. "You show me tomorrow," he said.

My father attracted wounded animals. Once we were out shooting targets with .22s. We'd shoot, and our father would make a remark. "Higher, lower, a little to the right, or to the left," he'd say. We told him we could see perfectly well. "Of course," he answered, "it's just a matter of practice." So we'd shoot and shoot and shoot. Once he wasn't commenting. Linda and I turned around to find our father holding his arms out and staring up to the sky as if he expected something to fall. It did. It fell from the sky right into my father's arms. It was an eagle. "The sign of America," our father said. It had been shot, and it died in his arms.

·

We had never been to a party, but we had heard about them from books. You get dressed up and look happy. When my mother got a job at Pan Am, it seemed to my sisters, my father, and me that she was going off to a party. After a while she began to bring home little refrigerators. We would all gather around. She would show us beautifully shaped food that didn't taste good. She whispered whenever she showed us because they were surprises for our father. We wanted to keep the refrigerators, but she said she had to take them back.

He stood over the boat.

"It doesn't leak much," I assured him. "Pam Richards came, see?" I pointed to her patch. She used the top of a tin can and pine pitch. He said it was a good patch but that he was worried about the rest of the boat.

"Get in, Daddy." I pushed him out through the reeds. He let me row.

"Water," he said, looking down between his feet.

"Here." I handed him a coffee can. "Just use this." It was perfect—he bailed, I rowed.

I could row so the water made less sound than the wind or the sound of reeds. I missed the rocks. The sound of the river this time of year was low, so we didn't speak. We heard hawks and jays. We watched a bobcat look up from a patch of sunny moss on a rock. The sound of the world was all things taking fair turns, until my father said, "Look!" too loud and made a beaver slap the river with its tail and jays leave the pine trees and other sounds separate into parts. He knew what he had done. He bailed again and went quiet. The river was clearer than usual. He held the can still in water and watched fish investigate with their lips. In the distance I could hear the invisible women, held inside the glacier, singing their high soprano songs.

"Jesus, Susan!" my father called. I turned the boat so the bear wouldn't see my father. I made myself large and faced the animal. I held the oars up to keep the boat silent so we were just river. The grizzly left his long salmon on the rock and slipped back into the shadowy woods. My father took the oars from me. The river and the wind seemed to have picked up speed. Crows yelled.

We had a flesh-colored pickup truck. A Ford. Once my sister Linda decided she wanted to drive. The pickup started with a push button. She ended up in the river. My father had to get another truck to pull her out. Other things about the river frightened my parents. Once our youngest sister disappeared. She had just learned to walk. We looked all day. It was my mother who found her. She was standing at the river's edge, stuck to her chest in mud.

The operating room was not difficult to get into. If the door off the front entryway was locked, you could get in through the chicken coop in the back.

•

Another thing about the pickup. It had a deep glove compartment that was lined with felt, and because it was always so damp, the whole thing was soft. Linda and I enjoyed digging around in it. We'd take out the tools, open and close the pliers, wind up the monkey wrench, unfasten the leather pouch of the pickax, and take short blows with it at the air. Some of the things were more interesting than others. We figured in a place like that there had to be something to eat. All we could find that tasted good were lighter flints and lead washers. We left a few.

Linda and I first felt height when we learned how to shinny from a boy at school. We found limbless trees out near the smokehouse and shinnied up till they got too narrow. When the wind blew, our trees bent in half in slow motion. By leaning in certain directions we could draw imaginary lines in the air with our moving bodies. Eventually we could make full circles and write our names.

•

My father's best friend was hunting with his boys. They were attacked by a grizzly. One of the boys was blinded and had to be sent to the States to learn Braille. My father said the boat case was closed.

The first reason he gave for not allowing me to take the boat out anymore was the leak. So Patty and Linda and I pine-pitched the whole thing down. It didn't make a difference.

"But why then?" I asked. He didn't say anything. He just stood there squeezing his temple with one hand. He did not say it was because he was afraid of bears.

"But I'm not afraid!" I told him.

"That doesn't matter," he said.

"Why then?"

"Because I said so," he said, and turned away.

During the summers my father ran Obedience Training in the kennel in a large empty room. It was a new addition to the barn. At first it seemed like fun—

with its various loops, ramps, and sawhorses. But it was just another kind of operating room. Any dog who spent time in there could be ruined.

"What do you do that to them for?" I asked him.

"It's not me, it's my business," he said. "Some people want dogs who do what they say and nothing more."

"You shouldn't let them on our property then," I said.

He stopped in the middle of his circle and yanked back so hard on the choke chain that the golden he was walking coughed.

"Don't you have something to do," he said, "—look for signs or something?"

"Looking for signs" was an activity I did with my sister. We'd take the path behind the long house. It had numerous forks on it, often marked with Indian totem.

Once my mother had given us gum from town.

"Deer," my sister said, squatting down beside a

bone surrounded by fur. "Don't be sad." She looked up. "Maybe he'll change his mind about the boat when you're my age." I got down beside her.

"Did he say you could use the boat?"

"No," she said, and poked the bone with a long pinecone. "He said he was going to get rid of it."

"Let's go," I said. Linda accidentally dropped her gum on upturned fur and pine needles. She picked it up, then dropped it. I took mine out of my mouth. "Here," I said, and she took it.

We went off the path, and after several hours found a dead bear. We pulled out all its teeth and other loose bones. We carried them home in our jackets, which we made into bags—sleeves as handles.

People who came on to our property either brought ailing animals or bad news. Once someone brought a set of goats. No one in our family liked them. The dogs wouldn't stop barking at them. They were too unfriendly to milk, and they smelled terrible. The fence out in the front of the house was only one side to a possible square, but the only thing that kept it from being purely decorative was the gate at the center. It kept people on a particular path from the driveway to the front door. But the goats were tied to the gate, so everyone who exited or entered the house had to make a wide semicircle around the length of fence—goat, gate, and all. My father wanted to get rid of them because they attracted wildlife. One of my father's customers finally took them away, but even after they were gone the gate still smelled, so no one used it. The chickens also smelled. But they were so small and needed so much protection from wildlife I felt sorry for them way out in the back of the barn. Luckily the shed was big and they could roam around. I didn't spend much time out there because my father was raising them to eat, and he said he didn't want us turning them into pets. I began to watch. He had set a dog's leg the night before. It had been caught in a trap. The bleached operating rags were still drying on a sagging line in the shed. It was a sunny room, with a soft sawdust floor. Chickens clucked happily around my father's feet thinking he was going to give them grain.

My father's lips tighten when he concentrates. And he will not talk. "Why should we live here if I can't use the boat and go on the river?" I asked him. He didn't answer. He grabbed a chicken and held its neck to the log. "How can you get rid of that boat? WHY? Where will you send it?" The chicken got away. "Damit, Susan!" he said, chasing it. He slammed it down onto the log again and chopped off its head. The chicken dropped away from the log again and ran around. I had never seen this before. I screamed because the chicken was coming straight at me as if to say, "Find me my head!" My father tried to cheer me up later with its claw. He said, "Isn't this interesting?" and pulled some of the tendons in the wrist so the claw opened and closed.

He began digging a new hole for a bigger septic tank out in the field beside the house when my mother started working. He got very dirty and didn't want us casting our shadows over him. "Git outa my light, damit," he'd say.

Dampness in general was a big problem in Alaska. That's probably why my father kept his medical tools locked in glass cases. He was out digging in the mud. We wore identical green packs. The water was coming in over his pack as he shoveled. I had been in the operating room—no reason, just exploring. Everything was silent in there, and warm from incoming sun. My father cursed in the dark hole at rocks and gravel. In the room I had found several single-edged razor blades on the windowsill. No one had moved them for so many years they had rusted together into one shape. All but three. If he had been in the room with me, he would have said, "Git away from there." I sawed the inside of my thumb and filled my cupped hand with blood.

"Daddy," I said into the ground. He didn't know I was there. He threw the shovel down and stretched his back, maybe a little thankful to be taken away from this terrible task.

"Help me up," he said, reaching his hand up to me. I wanted to hide what I had done, but it was too late.

He cleaned up my hand in the kitchen sink. He didn't say anything. Dogs can bleed to death if you clip a nail too short. To stop the bleeding on a dog's nail he used styptic sticks. He used a styptic stick on my thumb. Then he used a butterfly bandage and a tongue depressor and gauze.

Out by the boat, in the shadows of cedar trees, a shrew ran into a hole between two massive roots. The dog whose belly I was using for a pillow under the boat chased it and began to dig. The bite from a shrew can make you sick, but I wanted to see its blind face and so did the dog. She dug and stood back to let me reach in. "More," I said to Lisa. Finally I felt the shrew and pulled it out. It got away. Lisa and I chased it for a while but lost it. I followed her back to the tree. We were standing there staring down at the opened entryway when my mother came up beside us. She said she had been looking for me. She wanted me to come inside. It wasn't going to get dark tonight, and I lost track of time.

Every night, and during bad weather, our mother read to us. That meant quite frequently in Alaska. She had a certain way of organizing the reading. She had to be beside the lamp, and we four girls had to rotate, taking turns sitting beside her. I wanted to sit beside her all the time or not at all. So I always sat farthest away. It had to do with the book illustrations. If I started the illustrations to a story she was reading at the far end of the couch in my imagination, and then had to move midstory up beside her only to find the pictures I came up with didn't match the illustrator's, I'd lose all concentration on the story. So I sat at the end of the couch most of the time, unless she read a documentary with photographs or renderings. To make up for time apart, my mother spent extra time with me when she tucked us in. She'd do everyone else then lie down with me. I'd watch her face's side view. She didn't look like me. She had brown eyes like the German shepherds' and raven-black hair. Her eyelids were almost transparent. She would talk with her eyes closed. Often she would fall asleep while I wrapped the curly ringlets of her hair around my fingers.

Sometimes it rained for months and months without stopping. During these times, and for days after, the river would change considerably. The reeds would be flooded over, the water would be turned into a brown-gray mud. It often rose so high it would go over the bridge to the driveway, so we were trapped. Once after an especially long rain, my mother dressed us in our rubber clothes and sent us out. "Stay away from the river," she said. Linda took the younger ones to play upstairs in the barn on the equipment. I listened to rain drip from trees onto the metal hood of the pickup while lying on the front seat. It was as if each drop said, "Where have you been," and had come to

21

see me. I sat up and watched the water rush down the river. It wasn't our river this time of year. It was another river who had invaded our property. It just needed to get through one way or another. It was big and in a hurry. But somewhere underneath was a quiet, reedy river, with a red, silt bottom, spotted fish, and slippery stones under clear water. I took the pickax from the truck.

The wood was soft and covered with moss. It had been a long time. Red lichen and stone spiders fell around the split wood.

My father had to shoot dogs with hip dysplasia, a dislocation of the hips common in German shepherds. I remember his turning around after shooting Lisa. It was just after a rain.

I heard my name.

EARTHQUAKE

In Alaska all things are large. You can notice it by moving to Massachusetts and comparing seagulls, blueberries, squirrels, rhubarb, blue jays, or anything else that moves or grows. Blueberries in Massachusetts looked like something was wrong. I felt like I was eating sad food for a long time, like runts of the litter. Also, if anything was sent to Alaska from the States, it stood out in high contrast. Once our grandmother sent us a parakeet, but there was an earthquake. When the side of the house fell down in slow motion, we watched that little bird escape from its cage and fly off, over the leaning roof and high into the massive pine

23

limbs. We heard blue jays. We never saw that bright and delicate bird again.

One of my father's friends picked blueberries for a living. After the earthquake they only found her shoe. I asked my father if she got swallowed up, but I never got a straight answer. I figured either she got swallowed up or she used the earthquake as an excuse to run off with someone.

Our grandmother was pale and vulnerable. Her name was Mildred Elizabeth, and she wore nylons, even when she came to visit us in Alaska, all the way from Massachusetts. She didn't talk much and kept her hands folded most of the time.

One morning she asked me where I was going so early and all alone. I told her outside and asked her if she wanted to come. She didn't.

I took the boat out as far as the rapids, tied it up, and walked the rest of the way along the banks. Toward the end of June, after the eggs have been laid, for about three, four days, tiny tadpoles that form inside transparent casings begin moving to break free. It all happens at once. I took tin cans and filled them up with tiny frogs. Back at the house I dumped them into a pail and sat waiting for my father's customers. My father and my grandmother came over, across the wide gravel driveway, over the rock pile, in and out of sun, to where I was sitting on the kennel steps. He said, "They won't sell, Susan." My grandmother looked at him, and he went inside, through the door with the moose antlers over it. She gave me a dime and said she'd pick it up later, after supper. "Suppah," she said, "aftah suppah."

After we ate supper, talk about game and preparation started. I tried to get my grandmother's attention. "Would you like your frog now?" I asked. She ignored me. I must have said, "Would you like your frog now?" a hundred times. Nothing. I left the table and wandered around. My grandmother was leaving in the morning. I stood in my mother and father's dark room and held my grandmother's hat. It was a round, cupped hat with a long, pearl-tipped pin and a male pheasant's feather curled around its rim. I took the pin.

Back out in the light and the commotion I stood beside her, pin in one hand, frog in the other. I put the frog on her plate. I thought she saw me, and I thought she saw the frog. But she didn't look down, or say thank you, or tell me she would not go. She kept her hands folded and smiled at my parents as they talked. I pushed the pin into her thigh not too hard. She jumped, but she did not make a sound. I must have hurt her. Her eyes were full of tears, but she said, "It's quite all right" so I would not get into trouble.

Going home with kids after school in Alaska was unpredictable. One day I got permission to go home with an Indian girl named Johanna. I remember high fences and reindeer. We went into domed huts. I asked her what things were used for, things fastened to the walls. She told me, but she talked so fast I could not make out the words. I was there only for the afternoon. We ate fish from skunk-cabbage leaves. Later we talked under the reindeer.

Reindeer have incredibly large nostrils. They have soft, light, short hairs on their snouts. They have round, dark eyes. They lower their heads, then tilt them to one side and look at you from one eye when you are up close. They flick their ears when you whisper. Johanna said she was tired of the reindeer, "Let's go, let's go," but my mother came.

I remember Johanna standing with her family on the other side of the fence. My mother waved to her family. Johanna waved to me. Her family waved to both of us. I waved to the deer.

My father taught himself all about dogs. I'm not sure when it all started, but he was very thorough, and in Alaska he sent to the States for books—books on dog diseases, vividly illustrating how to take care of certain problems, both mundane and amazing. It got him started on the Tongas Dog Ranch, where he bred and boarded dogs, mostly German shepherds. "You start with the best," he said, so we got Rin Tin Tin's cousin and named him Nocturne of Tongas Forest. My father was particular about names. He couldn't understand how any person could name their child Lisa, Tammy, Kim, Maggie, or Duchess. These were the names of our females. He didn't have much to say about naming males. Ours were Buck, King, Star, Nocky, etc. The leaders were Nocky and Lisa, King and Duchess. In the wilderness they could make you feel important just by walking beside you. I had seen them chase bears away and form themselves into a ring.

Sometimes after two or three weeks if a missing dog did not return, my father would take his gun to who-knows-where to look for it. If they didn't kill, bear traps could break a leg, so that even my father, who was thought to be an expert vet, couldn't get it to work right. Sometimes he'd have to shoot them, but he'd bring the bodies home. We would know right away what had happened if we saw a bundle in the back of the pickup between rattling bear traps. If it was still alive, it'd be up front with its head on my father's lap. Trappers setting up on our land made my father so mad he'd stop talking.

The kennel smelled like experiments and blood. When it was my turn to feed the injured ones, I'd make it real quick. They wanted to get up when they saw me because they didn't want to be seen that way, but they couldn't. They fell back down and looked away. It was a secret they wanted to keep with my father. I'd dump the Purina into their pans, hose them some water, and avoid their eyes.

After they healed, we could tell them apart by the sounds of their various limps at night on the linoleum floors. We could hear them moving room by room, the sound increasing as they moved closer.

If you laid your head on their bellies, you could

hear planets colliding, and glaciers falling in great sheaths of ice. My father said, "Nonsense, it is only because they have seven more digestive chemicals than we have."

Once in a while there were masses of sluggish fish in our creek. They were so sluggish the dogs could wade in and, without any effort, bring them back to us. Most of our dogs spent their time pulling fish out of the water. I thought this was why they were called dog salmon. Later I learned it had nothing to do with our dogs and that they were too mushy to eat unless smoked. That's probably why my parents left most of them lying around and why our smokehouse was constantly burning. There were so many dog salmon in the river that my sisters and I could reach in and run our hands down the fishes' backs. They were long and sleek and would not swim away. Looking out the high window in the house at all those fish, skin shimmering under the moon, I asked my father what had happened. He said they had finished their lives and chosen our place to die, and then he smiled as if we should all feel very lucky.

Various buildings on our property were not used. Besides the house, the barn, and the smokehouse, there were the longhouse beyond the stone field, the mink runs behind the barn, and the utility shed behind the house. My father put moose antlers over the barn door and built new steps for the house, and the smokehouse was always burning. The other buildings begged my sisters and me for our attention.

The mink runs had fallen to one side and then to the other and were sometimes folded on to themselves. We never locked one another inside the cages because we smelled the animals, and even though we never saw any, we felt them. Playing around the mink runs never lasted long and made us quiet. But the longhouse was a generous and appreciative place. It was kept locked but slanted its roof down on one side just low enough for the stepladder we found in the thorny bushes to reach it.

My sisters and I were not often responsible for one another. We went our separate ways, but sometimes our mother asked Linda and me to keep an eye on the younger ones, Wendy and Sandra. We had been told not to go near the building with the slanted roof when once our mother had found us up there on the peak. But that was years ago, and we had been up there so many times since, we figured she had made a mistake with her request. So we hoisted the little ones up ahead of us and called the dog up, too, to keep it from barking. We said, "Come on Lisa, come on," and it limped up the ladder.

We sat in a line on the top of the building, held up to see the world. A good building, I thought, for this. There were the mountains, sharp and blue and white, and the hawks over the river. A ribbon of smoke eased up from the house and curled over the tips of the trees. We sat still in the cool wind. The sun moved down, turning the sky red. In the distance we could hear one of the dogs barking at a fish, and the high whine and low rumble of the glacier, and the movement of the forest, and way off, the sound of our mother calling. It was a strange cry that increased the sound of the wind and lowered the temperature and made us grip the peak of the roof as if it were the edge of the planet. We looked down at her. She looked awful, but she tried to smile. She helped us down. The stones in the field seemed to have grown sharper, and the field to have expanded, and it took us a long time to get home.

My mother used to take me places driving. I didn't know or care where. She liked to drive down roads and explore. And she said she just wanted to see another human being that was not related to our family. We looked at houses and at cliffs, then we would sit in someone's kitchen or living room and have conversation, or she would. I would rather be moving road by road.

Once she took me for a long ride to the hospital because I had to have my tonsils out. The hospital was small. After it was all over and she had taken me home, we had to turn around and go back the next day because I began to hemorrhage from my throat. New snow was still falling. It glistened on the windshield. I wanted to be outside catching the flakes with my tongue. Instead I was inside the pickup leaning over a pail. We stopped at the Richardses', and she left me in the truck. I listened to her feet on the snow, the snow against the metal hood, to the sound of her telling them to send their oldest back to stay with my sisters. My father was out on a hunt. She drove in reverse down their long driveway. Back on the road she touched my head. Periodically my mother would have to empty the pail. I could sometimes sit up and see the red spray out onto the white snow in the light of the high beams. She slipped the pail back between the stick shift and the seat and slammed the door.

There was no A-positive at the hospital, and I passed out. My mother and the doctors told me later they had put an announcement on the radio and a small plane had landed in the parking lot. They told me I was part pilot. It was my birthday, that day of the transfusion. My mother gave me an Indian doll. A few days later I saw an Indian woman in one of the rooms down the hall and went in to show her my doll. She asked me what its name was. I told her it was Linda, for my sister. Later when my mother had fallen asleep with her head on my bed, a nurse came in with a feather and told me it was from the Indian woman. I stuck it into my mother's hair.

My parents hardly ever sat together on the living room couch. It was a green couch, a heavy green couch, with wood arms. The shoulders drooped downward, so it had the appearance of being sad. When the family sat together on it, it seemed to change expression.

Once we were called together there, and our parents told us they were getting divorced, and then they told us what the word meant. There were four girls, and we were divided up evenly. My little sisters were to stay with my mother, since she knew more about diapers. Linda and I were scheduled to leave for Massachusetts with our father on Saturday by plane.

I had never seen a plane before. They packed our things in matching suitcases. It was 1958. It was the last I saw of Alaska. The following year it was made a state.

We arrived in Massachusetts in the middle of the night. My father's sister met us at the airport. She was waiting in a car by glass doors. I saw her first from behind. She was part of the flashing lights, the colored words outside, and the darkness. On the steering wheel I saw her fingers, painted and narrow. When she turned the car one way or another through the lights, she would lift her fingers up, stretch them out, and curl them back around. Once, when the car was stopped, she turned around. She had a nice smile like my grandmother's, but her eyelids were turquoise and reminded me of reptiles, so I had to look at her from the nose down.

Grandparents do not use words in usual ways. I had to walk back home to their house every day after school in terrible heat. Once I stuck my face under the kitchen faucet and let the cold water run over my hair, my eyes, in my mouth, like a miniature waterfall. My grandmother interrupted me and said, "You don't do that!" I said, "Yes I do," because I just did, that was plain enough to see. But after some time I realized that the "you" my grandmother meant was not me, but the rest of civilization.

The first time I saw TV was in the morning. *The Three Stooges.* I asked my uncle how it worked. He said electrically. He sat very still. I asked him what exactly happens. He said the men act out in one place in front of a special camera that sends their picture in the form of frequencies into the air. He said the house picks them up through the antenna. He had to say it over and over because the Three Stooges were making so much noise. I had to sit still to understand them. When I got out of the stillness I looked back at my uncle to see if he wanted help getting out, but he was smiling.

I used to spend a great deal of time in front of the bathroom mirror making grotesque faces. I developed the habit when I was ten. A bad year. At ten I learned that by sitting with my head between my knees, folded in half on the footstool, I could fall asleep immediately. That same year Alice Stanton beat me up because I did something wrong in football, and Kathy O'Brien, who used to walk me home from school, decided to dump me for Richie Dagistino. She said she wanted to use her time for making out with Richie under the viaduct after school. So I had to learn to walk home alone. I began running at first out of fear, but eventually I became a good runner and won the regionals at school.

For a while my father had to work for someone else. His name was Russ Fuller. It was my father's job to deliver tropical fish for Russ Fuller's Afmar Supply Company. He worked from a blue van, and occasionally he felt sorry for me and took me with him. My father was often a cheerful man. He could yodel and keep a cigarette in his mouth at the same time.

The Afmar Supply Company had a warehouse behind the front office. The warehouse was dark to cut down on the buildup of algae. The front office was bright. When Russ Fuller was not in the back, he was in there, on a swivel chair between a girlie calendar and a gray metal desk. The fluorescent light buzzed and flicked. It was not regular.

The back room was a city of aquariums. You could

get lost between the rows of tanks. My father knew exactly where to go for tetras, neons, mollies, and angels. He knew a lot about fish. He told me where their real homes were. I kept comparing places like Africa and Brazil to the Afmar Supply Company.

"Come here," he said once, and took my hand and walked me down to the darkest range of the warehouse to a tank the size of a coffin. He turned the lamp on over the top. We pressed our faces against the glass. "Piranha," he said. "Meanest fish in the world. Just look at those undershot jaws." He told me that a long time ago Russ Fuller had thought they had all died and had stuck his hand in there to see how thick the algae was and had gotten his finger bitten off. He said it must have been mice falling off the pipes and into the tank that kept the fish alive. On the way out I asked Russ Fuller a number of questions about tropical fish. Finally he pulled his hands out from under his desk to show the curving shape of a particular fin, and you could see very clearly, one of his fingers was missing.

•

Propaganda was a big issue at the Waltham Junior High. You could just get under your desk and hold your head for the bomb warnings, but for films on propaganda it was difficult knowing what to do. Unfortunately it was a new school, and I didn't have any friends, so by the end of the year I suspected everyone. I saw all things and events in terms of propaganda, but especially the films themselves. After learning so much about the dangerous and powerful effects of propaganda on an individual and even a nation, and after seeing film clips on all the various methods used for control, from bandwagon to brainwashing, I decided to be careful in the way I used my eyes.

Though the films were mostly in cartoon form, it was obvious the United States was using the same techniques on my classroom that they were simultaneously accusing the Communists of using against our country. So, in order to avoid being propagandized, I developed a way to watch such films and not be systematically manipulated and ultimately controlled by them. I never looked directly at the film with the center of my eyes. I looked at the film and at the heads of the people in the room at the same time, and I was never carried away by the story. I would be reminded of where I was exactly. I used my sideways vision. I looked at somebody's shirt and saw the film in the same frame with no more or less focus. It was shirt, hair, shades, chalkboard, film, sweater, hooks, ear, etc. That way a booming voice saying words like "total control, information, agencies, international, dissemination," or "warfare," meant no more than "gimmie that note," or "I'll tell," or "got any more gum?" It was like listening to a forest. The film was just another tree.

I did not have friends, whereas my sister had both friends and organizations. She excelled in her subjects. She was in the Latin Club and the English Club. I had to do my best just to show up at school every day. My sister was beautiful and matured early. I walked on the other side of the street to avoid contrast. I had a hard time even looking at my classmates. If they saw Linda, they'd come right over and ask questions and never seemed to go away. Linda swore her high school teacher had a crush on her. Later, after he published his books, she swore she was in them. It was a combination, she told me, of her character and others. She would come home every day after school with reports on Gregory McDonald.

Sometimes my sister asked me to help her study. I remember "pun." "What is pun?" I asked. "The truth couched in obscurity," she answered. I asked her what that meant. She said, "That's not part of the question." Then she said, "Well maybe it's crouched . . . the truth crouched in obscurity." But either way, it made no sense to me, so I never forgot it.

She often took advantage of our differences. She read to me parts of *Portnoy's Complaint* and *Candy* to disgust me, then she gave me D. H. Lawrence and J. D. Salinger to cheer me up. She told me whom to avoid once I got to high school.

It didn't matter. I was so scared I wanted to break

my legs for good to keep from going. She said not to worry, but after the first day I realized she was wrong. I needed my legs for running, but I researched appendicitis, and one morning I woke up screaming. With my father's medical background, it all went very smoothly. He took me to the hospital, Clinton General. The doctors were serious. They took off my clothes and shaved me. They put me in a paper gown and wheeled me away from my father. They knocked me out. When I woke up there was a long-faced doctor leaning over me. He said, "We got it just in time. And look, I put the incision low enough so that you can still wear a bikini."

That gave me one whole week away from home and three from school.

My father was a big sneezer. He went through elaborate gestures to get the handkerchief out of his back pocket before it actually happened. Once, during one of our tense, silent Sunday drives, when we were all sick from too much traveling, he sneezed explosively.

He let out a great sigh afterward. It was an extraordinarily timed sneeze, giving us all a resurgence of energy.

"Did you know," he said, "that every time you sneeze your heart skips a beat?" Then he calculated how many times he sneezed per day on the average, then per week, and onward to per lifetime. He calculated that by the age of ninety he would have been already dead for two and a half hours. "Isn't that fascinating?" he said.

There were other things that fascinated my father. Once when we were all lying around on chaise longues, facing a hot sun with closed eyes, he said, "Listen!" We sat up, straddling our chairs, and turned to face him. He gripped his forehead the way you do when you have a migraine. He squeezed his temples together. We all heard it . . . a kind of grinding crack. Then he took a flat hand on the front of his head and another on the back. There it was again—the same crack. "Isn't that interesting," he said, and lay back down.

CALLING HOME

At first I thought the house our father took us to after the divorce had a fire alarm in it. During our welcoming dinner, which was silent, some kind of bell rang out, making everyone sit up straight. I was listening for someone to announce which door to exit when my aunt stood up and said, "I'll get it." After dinner my sister and I were invited to view the telephone. It had its own shiny table at the base of a spiraling staircase. Our grandmother said, "And you must never forget your number." This was our number: BI4-5330.

Compared with Alaska, houses in that neighborhood were close together. It would seem you could stand on a porch and with only a slightly raised voice have a conversation with a neighbor to the left, the right, or across the street. Not so. Every time I went to the porch with the excuse to feed Chipper, my grandmother's squirrel, who was kept in an earwig-infested cage out there, no one else was around. Our house had rough, gravelly shingles and heavy cream-colored railings. It was bargelike to me, a ship with a heavy load, and it seemed peculiar not to wave if I spied another person there. Miss Mooney, who wore a bun and worked for an oil company, lived on one side. On the other was Mrs. Libby, whose overweight miniature collie ended up biting my grandmother's leg. They eventually began to wave back. "But," my grandmother told me, "it makes no difference." We could not go exploring their front yards and backyards, and we had to be invited to see the insides of their houses.

Restrictions were placed on streets by families. There were few friends to choose from in my area, but I thought of Mark Burns because his last name sounded like mine and we lived on the same street. But Mark did not think that mattered and chased me away with a log. Later I met Timmy Cook, who looked just like Timmy in *Lassie Come Home*, but his father was a missionary and they had to move away to India. Sissy and Brother McMullen's mother made me pray when I visited, and Beth Ellen's yard was too full of bees. I thought of my mother saying with her hands, "Here's the church, here's the steeple, open the door and see all the people."

My grandmother suggested the Congregational Church on Main Street, which seemed perfect to me, but my father was opposed. He said he was raising his kids to believe in the will not the rules and that we would go to the Unitarian Church.

"But," I said to my father, "that's a brick church. I want to go to a church with a steeple." And luckily my grandmother told him, "She can believe in anything she wants, wherever she wants, so long as she keeps her mouth shut about it," so he let me go. Unfortunately when I got there the front door was locked. A man with a hose told me I had to enter through the side door, down the end of the stone stairwell, and the woman sitting at a desk inside said the same thing. On Sundays, she told me, I would have to be accompanied by an adult in order to use the main entrance. I never went back.

My family had Russian friends in Alaska who lived on a rugged bluff overlooking the wildest part of the ocean. The Gitkoffs. They had seven children, and when we'd visit, my sister and I ran with them around those cliffs. I remember falling in a muddy field full of bulls where my boots got sucked off. All the Gitkoffs were on the other side of the fence screaming, "Watch out! Get up! Run!" and, "Don't move or else they'll kill you," or "Oh, no! She's wearing red!" We ran down pinecone paths racing against one another as if being outside was some kind of contest. They yelled to me that if I wanted to see things I had to keep up.

One of the things I saw with the Gitkoffs was the underwater shrine. There was such a big difference between where the water was when the tide was out and where it was when it was in, that the shrine, built on the edge of the sea, was underwater half the time. So when we made our way over the slippery stones of the spiral staircase, we found Jesus, hanging on a cross covered with starfish, which made him look surprised.

Chipper had an interior room to his cage. It was my job to make sure he had newspapers, which he shredded and pulled inside that dark room to cover himself with. It was also my job to carry the garbage out into the backyard and place it in a can located below the earth. Between rows of blossoming flowers there was a lever to step on, which lifted the lid to a concrete pit. It was always crawling with bugs. The other job I had was to take empty cans down to the cellar to my grandfather's studio.

My grandfather was mostly smells in the beginning. Turpentine, paint, pipe tobacco, and wood. Sometimes whiskey. Then he was sound. He used to swim with the man who played Tarzan in the movies. Johnny Weissmuller. He had developed the habit of blowing outward when he concentrated in the same way he would doing the Australian crawl. So frequently did he breathe this way that everyone called him Put. But then, it might have had something to do with his middle name, Putnam. Hiram Putnam. There were also the sounds of the shortwave radio he used for weather reports and fishing conditions, of ball games, and of table saws and hammering. And after some time, there was the sound of his voice as he talked with me.

"You don't want to paint a tree in a way it does not grow," he said. "And if you break a finger, fix it yourself with a stick, otherwise you end up with one that looks like this." He had a finger that hooked like a claw. "Or else make sure you make it useful," he said, demonstrating how it looped conveniently around a brush.

My grandfather painted signs and canvases. His subject matter had to do with men in natural settings. For example, he had several paintings of men fishing and of men pulling their boats in from lakes. He got his ideas from photographs of the family or from *Sports Illustrated* or *Angler Magazine* or from his father's sketchbooks, which he kept in a gray metal file cabinet. His signs were mostly white and blue letters on a field of battleship gray. He used big sheets of plywood framed in elaborate moldings, and he worked on sawhorses looking down. Before the words, the gray was a deep sea of moving space. It was anywhere and anything. I thought it was a good idea to hang signs without letters outside because they were more fun to look at.

After my grandparents moved to the Cape, his signs began to change. Less gray, more cutout shapes. I remember the sign for Pilgrim Road. It was a post with names of people pointing to the various dunes and off to the side, on an arm of its own, a pilgrim with a dead turkey slung on his back. Instead of a picture, it was a shape, held in a rectangular frame so the sky that would have ordinarily been paint, from a certain angle, was the sky around that road. I tried to explain to my grandfather what he did and why it was so clever, but he said, "Nonsense." He did it so the wind could get through and the sign would not blow over and fall into the cranberry bog.

My sister and I had to go live with our father when he married Marian, the IBM keypuncher from Raytheon. They got a place in Waltham in the Prospect Hill projects, an all-brick complex with concrete yards, front and back. We went to Plympton School, where my father had gone when he was our age, and we had the same sixth-grade teacher. It was Mrs. Patty, and her specialty was figures of speech.

Linda was in grade ahead of me and could tell me

about teachers to come. My father and Linda laughed because Mrs. Patty was still teaching the same things.

"Do they still call her Fatty Patty?" my father asked my sister. They did. I asked them why they made fun of her. They said it was because the figures of speech drove them crazy.

"What is a figure of speech, anyway?" I asked.

"It's a saying that makes communication clearer," my father said. I looked forward to Mrs. Patty's class and to a time when I could use a figure of speech.

Mrs. Patty enjoyed asking her class what certain things meant before she explained them.

"All the way around Robin Hood's barn," she said. No one could guess what it meant. She had an elaborate explanation, and we listened carefully, but it didn't help. I didn't understand it then, so I don't remember it now. I understood "in the doghouse" and "being neither here nor there." Unfortunately, in the classroom, I had such difficulty interpreting most of the sayings and got so many of them mixed up, that when I had the opportunity to use one I'd end up overexplaining it.

"Say, for example," I explained, "you were very small and were being eaten by someone or something very large. There was a fire outside and you were in a frying pan being cooked." My father wiped his mouth with his napkin and set it down beside his plate. "And in a moment's thinking you would say to yourself—"

"Susan!" my father interrupted, "we are talking about why you skipped school. Stick to it."

"Not only that," my stepmother interjected, "she's weaseling out of this one just like all those other times." She smoked thin cigarettes with decorations on the tip that ended up getting obliterated by her lipstick.

My sister looked at me. That's all she had to do. I knew what she meant: *Marian's never even* seen *a weasel!*

I know, I said to my sister with my face.

"Why?" my father said. "Why do you do this? You can't afford to skip your classes!"

"Well," I tried to explain, "it's sort of like standing in a big pan, thinking . . ."

"Frankly," he said, "I'm worried about you."

"Why? It makes sense, I mean I was in a kind of situation."

"You're damned right," he said.

"It's a figure of speech."

"Oh, listen to Miss Smart," Marian said. My father spun around and told her to be quiet.

I thought, *Oh, no!* and so did Linda, that was clear. I had just done what I said. Or what I was trying to say.

Also, Mrs. Patty had a peculiar way of singing. She took a big breath between syllables instead of between phrases, or words even.

"My (breath) cunt (breath) tree (breath) tiz

(breath) of (breath) thee," she sang in the front of the classroom. It was confusing, especially if you didn't know the song. At first I found it interesting. You had to think fast, listen carefully, and remember well in order to decipher meaning. I thought, this is great fun, and later, I was singing to my father and stepmother. It seemed more interesting to sing than to speak sometimes. More opportunity with breath and intonation to communicate. So I sang. During one of my singing times I found direct communication tedious, so I breathed between syllables the way Mrs. Patty did and found they paid attention to me. They had to listen forward in time and ended up actually looking at me, in an almost studying way.

People were always chasing other people for one reason or another around Prospect Hill. Sometimes it was hard to figure out why. I liked the new kid from Russia in our school. Russia is on the same latitude as Alaska, and he reminded me of the Gitkoffs. But one day he chased me, and when he caught me, he shoved leaves down my back and rubbed my face with mud. When I told my father, he laughed. He said it was the male way of showing affection. Another time I was going up one of the concrete hills between chain-link fences when a group of boys chased me with a long two-by-four, which they pounded into my chest until I could not breathe right. That's about the time we moved to Cherry Street near the Waltham Watch Factory and when my father switched from working with tropical fish to poodles.

My father told me when he was my age he couldn't take one more day of school so he pretended he was older and ended up in the Seabees, which somehow got him to Japan. He learned Japanese from the woman he lived with on a fishing junk before the navy found him, brought him home, and made him an interpreter. That is why when we got three poodles they had Japanese names. Skoshi, Chisai, and Shibu. I remember having to walk Skoshi. He was so hyperactive and pulled so hard on the leash, he ended up on his two hind legs, hopping down the street coughing and choking. The other two dogs' teeth fell out from chattering so much.

Everyone started carrying knives in Waltham Junior, and chains and brass knuckles. One of the boys in my homeroom swung at the teacher but missed, so his hand went through the blackboard and he had to have stitches. Eddie Elfar, who wore his shirt undone and lifted his collar, sat in front of me. During the commotion he stood up. I thought he was going to jump in and start fighting, but he turned around and pulled me off to one side of the room. I looked at him. He said he didn't want me to get hurt and that was the first time I felt love. But then we had to move again. This time to the country.

"Massachusetts's countryside isn't really nature anyway," I said to my father from the back seat of the car.

"It's private property." I suggested that if he really wanted to get back to nature, we just move back to Alaska, but he had Ye Old Poodle Shoppe now, he said, and things had changed. So we rented a small house with bad plumbing in the country, and he expanded his shop to include exotic pets.

As soon as he had my grandfather paint "and Exotic Pets" on his sign, people from all over Boston began bringing him pets they no longer wanted. My father would stand there in his shop, holding someone's iguana while they explained they had no idea how big they got. He ended up with skunks that hadn't been completely de-scented, birds that cursed, armadillos that would not unroll, and other animals whose problems it was difficult to determine. Sometimes my father would bring an animal home.

Once our family stood over a cage that took up half the front hall. A chimpanzee. I liked the idea of having an animal that made eye contact, but it reminded me of a time I had visited Benson's Wild Animal Farm and stood outside the gorilla cage with all the other people from my school watching. The gorilla made strange mouth contortions, peed, then sucked it up, and, with full cheeks, scanned the audience.

I knew the chimpanzee was going to pick me before it even happened, but there was no time to do anything about it. So, just in case, I stood behind my sister in the front hall as much as possible.

"What's the matter with this one?" Marian asked. The chimpanzee began to pick its fingernails.

"Supposedly it's vicious," my father said. "It's very young. A baby really."

For several months the chimp stayed with us. It would hop onto our backs when Linda or I did the vacuuming. It got into things, which made everyone laugh. Marian put it in diapers to keep it from wrecking the house. But one day it would not get off my back. It attacked me, biting me and tearing my shirt.

61

Linda and Marian ran around me like bees until someone finally thought of a blanket and got him off. From then on, until the day my father took him away from the house, he snarled and cried out at me every time I passed his cage, which was by the front door, so it was every time I'd come or go.

One day I took a bus to visit my grandmother. It was when they still lived in West Newton. I found her sniffling in the kitchen. She said it was because Chipper had bitten her. She opened the bandage on her leg to show me the wound. It wouldn't have been so bad, but it was in the same spot Mrs. Libby's dog had bitten her the month before. So she and my grandfather had taken Chipper to Boston Commons and left him there. "You can only keep something in a cage for so long," she said, wiping her nose with a hankie with orchids dyed into it. "We put him on a low branch of a tree, turned our backs, and left."

But after a few days they went back and found

Chipper on the same branch. Thinner. So they brought him home and made him a much more interesting cage with a hollowed-out tree trunk in it and a wire mesh on the bottom to help with the earwig problem.

The well finally dried up completely in that country house, and we had to move. My father and Marian bought a house on Willow Road in Berlin. It looked like a haunted-house cartoon, but it wasn't funny and my father agreed. The family who had lived there before us took off because they were in some kind of trouble, and my father found guns all over. There were hooting cries in the attic, which was locked from the other side, so we couldn't investigate. We had to take everything out of the house and burn it in bonfires in the back field. The basement was empty from the start, except for spiders and a freezer in one of the corners. One day my sister and I were helping Marian carry trash out for burning when our father came out with two plastic pails. We gathered around him while he pried off the lids.

"What is it?" Marian asked.

"I don't know," he said, "some kind of meat from the basement freezer." My father figured someone was chopped up. You could tell by his expression. He told us not to touch it.

In the morning we were awakened by our father calling us outdoors. He said, "Take a look at this!" He lifted the lids to the buckets. Beautiful multicolored beetles ran around on the inside, otherwise the pails were empty. "Undertaker beetles," he said. "Took care of everything."

"Oh, no!" I cried. "Now we'll never know what it was!" My father, Marian, and my sister looked at me as if to say "so what."

One night after the house was emptied and we had been stripping and painting walls all day, we were sitting on boxes in what was to be the living room when we heard that sound in the attic again. My father took a hammer, a crowbar, and a flashlight and said, "That's it. Let's go!" The house was in the shape of an L, and after prying open the attic door and creeping up the narrow staircase, we weren't exactly sure where we were in the sense of what was beneath us. With the flashlight we viewed what seemed to be a wall-less darkness. Unending. We stood suspended in it while my father's weakening battery light searched wildly, mothlike. He decided he had better take a look at this in the morning when he could see better. We never heard that cry again. My father said it was some kind of owl, either screech or barn.

Sun poured in from small windows between the peaks of the attic roof the morning he and I went up there to check things out. There were little porcelain knobs on the walls. When he pulled them, doors opened to dark empty rooms. In one room there was a small stained cot surrounded by beans, the kind you make chili with. And at the other end of the attic on a windowsill there was a circle of beans, something you would do while waiting for a door to open.

"Someone was here," I said to my father, "someone was locked inside." He pulled another knob.

"Look at this," he said. Another door opened to a room the size of a person lying down, but you could step over a short wall on the far end and get to the other side of the attic. "This is the addition," he said, "over the kitchen and the dining room."

"Was someone up here?" I asked him.

"Yes," he said.

"A prisoner?"

"No," he mumbled, "the lock was on the inside."

Our class took a trip once to the Museum of Fine Arts in Boston where we were asked to look closely at particular paintings. If you looked elsewhere, the guide would cough or say "Excuse me" or snap her fingers. I remember crowding in to discuss a portrait—a man with a pale face surrounded by a terrible unending darkness. We were then asked to hold up a thumb so it obscured the face. By doing this, the deep space around the sitter changed to paint. Flat, airless, impenetrable. It was just various shades of brushed-on black.

Otherwise, school trips involved visiting the homes of famous writers, clergymen, or politicians, which meant looking at antique furniture behind ropes.

Back roads are definitely free, but if you spend too much time leaning over a bridge to watch a creek take leaves under or reach your hand through a fence to touch a horse, you get the feeling that roads are also someone else's property. Someone was bound to come out of a house and say, "Can I help you?" as if the countryside were a department store. My father got telephone calls regarding my sister's and my answers to that question, even though all we said was no. Before long we were required to stay inside the house after school.

My sister told my father, "You can't keep us

cooped up in here. Everyone at school already calls us witches. Why can't we just be normal?"

"You tell me!" he said.

"What are we supposed to do?" we asked him. "Where are we supposed to go?"

"You're supposed to listen to music, I guess," he said, "in your rooms."

So Marian got us each a clock radio, and it wasn't until we got jobs at Northbrook Farms, a condemned ice-cream factory, that we went out onto those back roads again.

A person can develop friendship and communication with machines under the right circumstances. My sister and I were so good on the half-gallon machine that we were introduced to all the others, and it wasn't long before we looked forward to our afternoons after school in the factory despite the leaking pipes and the freezing water that filled our boots.

In the winter during breaks or if we got to work too early, which we most often did, we sat in the boiler room with the men drinking instant coffee with ice-cream mix. But in the summer we sat outside by a contaminated pond with a few discarded machine parts just behind the storage door. One time my sister went inside in the summer. Later, at the Dixie cup machine, she told me she was in love with Lannie, a twelfth grader who worked stock in the freezer. It got depressing sitting by that polluted pond week after week all alone, so I quit and got a job in Clinton at the Colonial Press, a book-packing factory where they gave employees who were good on machines imperfect copies of books they boxed. I got *The Chinese on the Art of Painting* for the pictures.

For some people it isn't easy to stay put in one place listening to someone else's interest when it isn't at all interesting. Except for Mr. Piergalini's writing class where we did J. D. Salinger imitations and Miss Mann's art class where we did anything we wanted and sometimes Mr. Little's Latin class because conjugating in long lists was a good excuse to experiment with what kind of handwriting you wanted to have, there wasn't much in school that compared with the outside.

Everyone had his or her own method. Linda would just cross the street before the bus came and hide between boulders in the cowfield. I'd take the bus in, drop off my books at my locker, and walk out the back door. Those with cars would just lie down in the seat until the last morning bell rang and wait for those who didn't.

Who was driving didn't matter. Most of the time I'd just jump in and pretend I knew someone. I just wanted to be in a car moving road to road. And if, after scanning the parking lot from the back door of the school, I didn't see a tail pipe that showed an engine idling, I'd just hitchhike to wherever. It ended up being good practice for later when I hitchhiked to Seattle and saw my mother, but at the time no one saw any value in those activities. So, when letters from the principal began showing up, my sister and I were no longer allowed to work afternoons and were restricted to our rooms.

My father said that when property isn't private because it's under the watchful eyes of neighbors it isn't really private property. So the land around our house was just a responsibility to him, like a domesticated animal with an occasional problem.

One day we discovered an escaped convict with a rifle who had set up a lean-to on our hill. He fit the description on our radios. So my father had to call the police.

"What if he's innocent?" my sister asked.

"They say he's dangerous and armed and we can't have him up there sitting with a gun," he said, "but I wish to hell he'd leave."

Afterward my sister said, "Well, at least now the police know we aren't witches," but my father felt differently.

"No! I don't know his name!" he snapped at her. "And sheriff or not, I don't like anyone snooping around here. What goes on here is our business."

Whenever I saw Donna with the ratted hair at school she was always with others, but the day she called me over to her locker she was alone. I had been in that school for a long time, and except for Jane and Gretchen, who were into dieting and death in the art room, no one talked to me.

"Yes?" I said.

"You know me. Right?" she said. "Everyone does. Anyway, how are you? You know I heard about you." She slammed her locker and accompanied me to my Latin class.

"That's impossible," I said, "no one knows me."

"From Lannie Kennedy?" she said. "I mean your parents." She seemed surprised that I was surprised, and for a minute I thought she was going to say never mind and walk away, but she didn't.

"I heard you aren't allowed to have any friends and

you can never go out, day or night, and they make you do all this work. You have nice eyes, ever use mascara? Anyway if you ever want to go around with us, lemme know, K?"

Once my sister and I were sitting on the roof trying to figure out what to do next when the phone rang and she went down to answer it. When she finally came back, she told me she had been accepted at a college in Washington State where our mother lived. Then we sang songs. We liked to sing outside. There was something in the wind that kept us harmonized and in tune.

My sister did not wait long after her graduation ceremony to leave. Just the time it takes to get to the airport in Boston by bus.

Airline companies used to let you trade in tickets for cash, no questions asked. I did that with the one my mother and sister sent me from Seattle.

I don't know why they call Buffalo "The Armpit of

the Nation," but I understand why Chicago is referred to as "The Windy City." Once I called home from a phone booth in a parking lot near Chicago. Afterward I ran back to the semi I was riding in and slammed the door. Wind shook the whole truck. That's how strong it was. And cold, too. When the driver got back inside with his fish fries and coffee, the windows steamed up immediately. I wiped out a spot on my side. A blue lake and a gray sky flicked by between buildings and posts. Part of the Great Lakes, I thought. Then there was the Great Divide. The Great Plains. Great Bend. Great Falls. Later, I was thinking out into the night about Great Pyrenees. My father had told me fossils of that breed of dog had been traced back to the Bronze Age. "They're guardians," he had said. I thought there must be something expansive about the Pyrenees, something significant, because of the "Great."

SUSAN BARNES

spent her childhood years in Alaska and in Massachusetts where she was born in 1950. She received her master's degree in fine arts in painting from the State University of New York at Buffalo in 1982 after several years of traveling with her two children, Ezra and Kate. From 1985 to 1991 Barnes taught at Cooper Union. In 1992 she moved to Pouch Cove, Newfoundland, and the following year to Missoula, Montana. Susan Barnes currently lives in Biddeford, Maine.